WOLFHOLD

STEVE BARLOW AND STEVE SKIDMORE
Illustrated by ANDREW CHIU

TITLES AT THIS LEVEL

Fiction

STUNT RIDERS
DAVID and HELEN ORME
978 1 4451 1314 2 pb

UNARMED AND DANGEROUS
DAVID and HELEN ORME
978 1 4451 1316 6 pb

WALK INTO DANGER
DAVID and HELEN ORME
978 1 4451 1318 0 pb

ROBBED!
ANNE CASSIDY
978 1 4451 1815 4 pb

WOLFHOLD
STEVE BARLOW and STEVE SKIDMORE
978 1 4451 1814 7 pb

WHITE WATER WIPE OUT!
ROGER HURN
978 1 4451 1816 1 pb

Graphic fiction

ALIEN CAGE
JONNY ZUCKER and NIK
978 1 4451 1322 7 pb

FUTURE TENSE
JONNY ZUCKER and LES EDWARDS
978 1 4451 1320 3 pb

THE DECIDERS
JONNY ZUCKER and ANDREW CHIU
978 1 4451 1324 1 pb

ASSASSIN CITY
JONNY ZUCKER and PEDRO J COLOMBO
978 1 4451 1803 1 pb

SWORD OF LEGEND
JONNY ZUCKER and COSMO WHITE
978 1 4451 1802 4 pb

SWITCH FACE
JONNY ZUCKER and KEV HOPGOOD
978 1 4451 1804 8 pb

Non-fiction

SUPER ANIMALS
ANNE ROONEY
978 1 4451 1358 6 pb

WORLD'S FASTEST
ANNE ROONEY
978 1 4451 1360 9 pb

GREATEST ROCK BANDS
ANNE ROONEY
978 1 4451 1310 4 hb
978 1 4451 1359 3 pb

SPACE
ANNE ROONEY
978 1 4451 1956 4 hb

DARING ESCAPES
ANNE ROONEY
978 1 4451 1957 1 hb

HOW TO SPEND A BILLION
ANNE ROONEY
978 1 4451 1955 7 hb

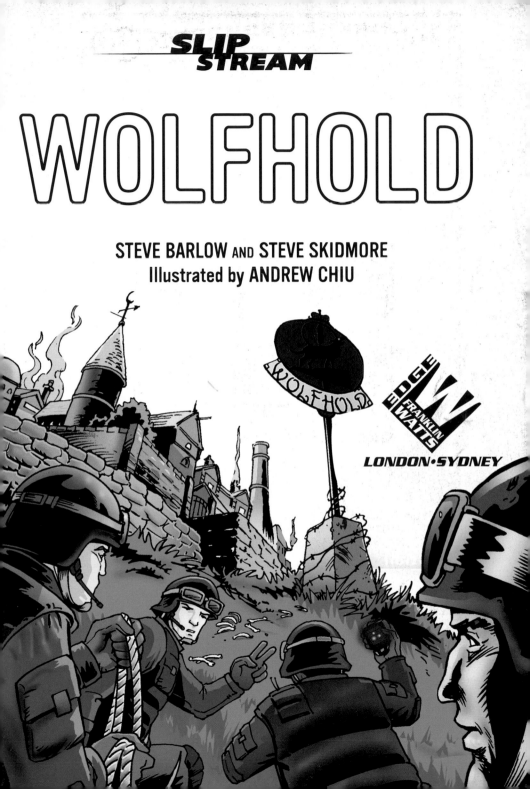

First published in 2013 by
Franklin Watts
338 Euston Road
London NW1 3BH

Franklin Watts Australia
Level 17/207 Kent Street
Sydney NSW 2000

A CIP catalogue record for this book is available from the British Library.

(ebook) ISBN: 978 1 4451 1820 8
(pb) ISBN: 978 1 4451 1814 7
(library ebook) ISBN: 978 1 4451 2606 7

Series Editors: Adrian Cole and Jackie Hamley
Series Advisors: Diana Bentley and Dee Reid
Series Designer: Peter Scoulding

1 3 5 7 9 10 8 6 4 2

Printed in China

Franklin Watts is a division of
Hachette Children's Books,
an Hachette UK company.
www.hachette.co.uk

CONTENTS

CHAPTER 1
A STRANGE PLACE

Tom woke up.

He was a strange bed...

...in a strange room...

...in a strange house.

Tom lived in London...

...but he was not in London now!

Tom ran out of the house.

He saw a girl.

"I'm Megan," she said.

"Do you know why you are here?"

"I don't know," said Tom. "I think there
was a fight but I can't remember."

CHAPTER 2
A STRANGE VILLAGE

Tom went into the shop.

He tried to buy a newspaper.

The shopkeeper shook his head.

"No papers in Wolfhold."

"Can I make a call or use the internet?" asked Tom.

"No phones or computers here," said the man.

"I want to go home," said Tom.

"Is there a bus out of here?"

"No bus," said Megan.

"What about a taxi?" asked Tom.

"No taxis," said Megan. "There's no way

out of Wolfhold."

CHAPTER 3
NO WAY OUT

Tom set off across the moor.

"There's no way out," called Megan.

But Tom kept going.

The road came to an end.

But Tom kept going.

Tom walked past a huge rock.

There were rabbits on the moor.

There were deer and goats.

But there were no roads,

and no people.

Tom came to a high fence.

He touched it.

"Aaargh!!"

He got a shock.

Then Megan was beside him.

"This is just the first fence. There are at least three more. No one has got past three."

"Come back to the village," said Megan.

Tom shook his head. "Why am I here?" he shouted.

"If only I could remember!"

CHAPTER 4
THE VILLAGERS

Tom followed Megan down the hill.

It was getting dark.

The moon was full.

They came to the huge rock.

The people of the village were

coming towards them.

"Soon you will understand," said Megan.

The villagers began to change.

Tom was scared.

"We have to get out of here!" he cried.

"Those people are werewolves!"

"I know," said Megan. "Welcome to the pack."

Then Tom remembered.

And he understood.

Wolfhold was the prison for his kind.

He would never leave Wolfhold.

WHITE WATER
WIPE OUT!

ROGER HURN

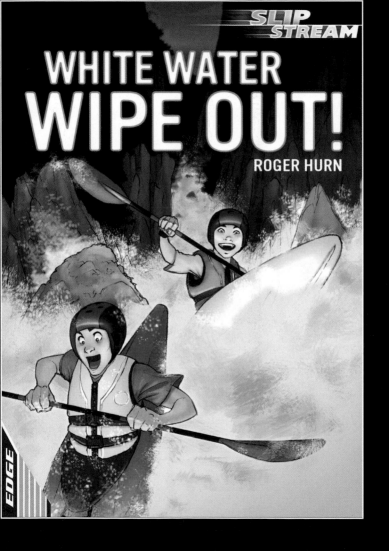

Rick and Ali are on a school trip.
They go white water rafting and it is brilliant!

Then Rick decides to try the out-of-bounds Hell Hole.
Will Ali be able to save his friend?

EDGE
FRANKLIN WATTS

LONDON•SYDNEY

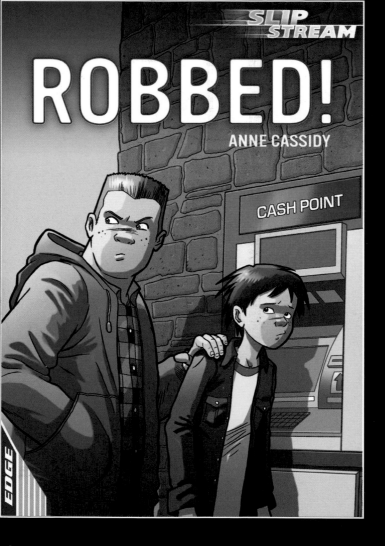

Tommy is late and his sister Lizzie is worried. She is told
that Big Alex is taking him to the cash machine.

Lizzie is sure that Tommy is about to be robbed.
What can she do?

LONDON·SYDNEY

FOR TEACHERS

About **SLIPSTREAM**

Slipstream is a series of expertly levelled books designed for pupils who are struggling with reading. Its unique three-strand approach through fiction, graphic fiction and non-fiction gives pupils a rich reading experience that will accelerate their progress and close the reading gap.

At the heart of every Slipstream fiction book is a great story. Easily accessible words and phrases ensure that pupils both decode and comprehend, and the high interest stories really engage older struggling readers.

Whether you're using Slipstream Level 1 for Guided Reading or as an independent read, here are some suggestions:

1. Make each reading session successful. Talk about the text before the pupil starts reading. Introduce any unfamiliar vocabulary.

2. Encourage the pupil to talk about the book using a range of open questions. For example, how else could the story end?

3. Discuss the differences between reading fiction, graphic fiction and non-fiction. What do they prefer?

Slipstream Level 1 photocopiable **WORKBOOK** ISBN: 978 1 4451 1798 0 available – download free sample worksheets from: www.franklinwatts.co.uk

For guidance, SLIPSTREAM Level 1 – Wolfhold has been approximately measured to:

National Curriculum Level: 2c
Reading Age: 7.0–7.6
Book Band: Turquoise

ATOS: 1.5*
Guided Reading Level: H
Lexile® Measure (confirmed): 110L

*Please check actual Accelerated Reader™ book level and quiz availability at www.arbookfind.co.uk